Welcome to ALADDIN QUIX!

If you are looking for fast, fun-to-read stories with colorful characters, lots of kid-friendly humor, easy-to-follow action, entertaining story lines, and lively illustrations, then **ALADDIN QUIX** is for you!

But wait, there's more!

If you're also looking for stories with tables of contents; word lists; about-the-book questions; 64, 80, or 96 pages; short chapters; short paragraphs; and large fonts, then **ALADDIN QUIX** is *definitely* for you!

ALADDIN QUIX: The next step between ready to reads and longer, more challenging chapter books, for readers five to eight years old.

Read more ALADDIN QUIX books!

By Stephanie Calmenson

Our Principal Is a Frog!
Our Principal Is a Wolf!
Our Principal's in His Underwear!
Our Principal Breaks a Spell!
Our Principal's Wacky Wishes!

Royal Sweets
By Helen Perelman

Book 1: *A Royal Rescue*
Book 2: *Sugar Secrets*
Book 3: *Stolen Jewels*
Book 4: *The Marshmallow Ghost*
Book 5: *Chocolate Challenge*

A Miss Mallard Mystery
By Robert Quackenbush

Dig to Disaster
Texas Trail to Calamity
Express Train to Trouble
Stairway to Doom
Bicycle to Treachery
Gondola to Danger
Surfboard to Peril
Taxi to Intrigue

Little Goddess Girls
By Joan Holub and Suzanne Williams

Book 1: *Athena & the Magic Land*
Book 2: *Persephone & the Giant Flowers*
Book 3: *Aphrodite & the Gold Apple*
Book 4: *Artemis & the Awesome Animals*
Book 5: Athena & the Island Enchantress

Little GODDESS Girls

Persephone & the Evil King

JOAN HOLUB &
SUZANNE WILLIAMS

ALADDIN QUIX

New York London Toronto Sydney New Delhi

ALADDIN QUIX
Simon & Schuster Children's Publishing Division
1230 Avenue of the Americas, New York, New York 10020
First Aladdin QUIX paperback edition January 2021

Also available in an Aladdin QUIX hardcover edition

For information about special discounts for bulk purchases, please contact
Simon & Schuster Special Sales at 1-866-506-1949
or business@simonandschuster.com.
The Simon & Schuster Speakers Bureau can bring authors to your live event. For more information or to book an event contact the Simon & Schuster Speakers Bureau at 1-866-248-3049 or visit our website at www.simonspeakers.com.
Cover designed by Tiara Iandiorio and Jess LaGreca
Interior designed by Mike Rosamilia
The illustrations for this book were rendered digitally.
The text of this book was set in Archer Medium.
Manufactured in the United States of America 1120 OFF
2 4 6 8 10 9 7 5 3 1
Library of Congress Control Number 2020935827
ISBN 978-1-5344-7963-0 (hc)
ISBN 978-1-5344-7962-3 (pbk)
ISBN 978-1-5344-7964-7 (eBook)

Cast of Characters

Circe (SEER•see): A beautiful but vain enchantress who lives on an island

Hestia (HESS•tee•uh): A small, winged Greek goddess who helps Athena and her friends

Heracles (HAIR•uh•kleez): A strong boy with dark, curly hair who carries a big, bumpy club

Queen: Rightful ruler of the island, imprisoned by King Hephaestus

Hephaestus (heh•FESS•tuss): An evil king who lives under a mountain on an island

Owlie (OWL•ee): A talking owl in magical Mount Olympus

Yellow Wing: The Owlie who travels to the island to help Athena find and free Heracles

Oliver (AH•liv•er): Athena's white puppy

Zeus (ZOOSS): Most powerful of the Greek gods, who lives in Sparkle City and can grant wishes

Contents

Chapter 1: The Quest Continues 1

Chapter 2: Into the Mountain 12

Chapter 3: Games 27

Chapter 4: Hidden Treasures 35

Chapter 5: The Silver Cane 57

Chapter 6: Journey's End 69

Word List 83

Questions 86

Authors' Note 88

The Quest Continues

"Too bad **Circe** wouldn't come with us," said **Persephone.** She and her friends, **Athena**, **Aphrodite**, and **Artemis**, had just left Circe the **enchantress**'s palace. They were on an island across the sea from magical **Mount Olympus.**

Athena had come from a far-away land. Magic had brought her to Mount Olympus where the other girls lived. During their first adventure together, a tiny flying **goddess** named **Hestia** had told them something amazing: They were all **goddess girls!**

Now Hestia had sent them and a boy named **Heracles** on a new quest: to rescue the **queen** of this island. An evil king named **Hephaestus** had captured the queen. She was trapped beneath the island's huge mountain!

Persephone gazed at the tall purple mountain in the distance. She wasn't sure how they'd be able to rescue the queen. But they would try.

"Yeah, Circe's magic could help us rescue the queen," said Aphrodite. "She could turn the evil king into a goose or something."

At this, Artemis flapped her arms and made honking noises. Everyone laughed.

"The king's magical powers are said to be **fierce**," said Heracles. "My club will best him, though." ***Swish! Swish!*** He swung his bumpy club in circles over his head. It was the size of a big baseball bat. He was about eight years old, the same age as the girls. And he was super strong.

"Hey, watch out!" said Athena, ducking his club just in time. A talking **Owlie** named **Yellow Wing** had been riding on her shoulder. It squawked and leaped out of the way.

Woof! Woof! barked **Oliver**. Athena's little white dog had been trotting alongside her.

"Oops! Sorry!" Heracles told them.

"What about my arrows?" Artemis flipped her black braid from one shoulder to the other. She nodded toward the **quiver** of silver arrows slung across her back. "If we have to battle the king and his army, they'll help too."

"Yeah. Speaking of helpful . . ." Athena looked at Aphrodite. "We'd get to King Hephaestus's mountain way faster if we had a **chariot**."

Aphrodite's blue eyes lit with excitement. "Ooh! Good idea!"

It really is! thought Persephone. But then Athena was super smart and full of bright ideas. Which was also helpful.

"Coo! Coo!" Aphrodite called to the sky. Right away a golden chariot pulled by beautiful white doves appeared overhead.

Persephone bent to sniff a red rose while they waited for the chariot to land. *Mmm*. She loved plants and flowers. In fact, she herself was part flower bush! Real leaves and flowers grew from her dress. And from her curly red hair, too, along with several four-leaf clovers.

Zeus had given her the clovers to bring her good luck. He was the most powerful of all the Greek gods.

He lived in a zigzag thunderbolt tower in **Sparkle City** at the top of Mount Olympus!

Plants and flowers loved Persephone just as much as she loved them. A touch of her fingers was enough to make them bloom more brightly. Sometimes they loved her a little too much, though. Once, some giant daisies had tried to capture her. They wanted to keep her as their friend forever!

Persephone ran to catch up with the others. She and Oliver

were the last ones to leap into the chariot. The doves took flight, pulling it into the sky.

"Wait for me!"

Yellow Wing called to the doves. He flapped off to join them.

The chariot circled over Circe's palace. Persephone saw hills, woods, shore, and sea. And across the sea, Mount Olympus. They headed in the opposite direction, toward the island's one mountain. Though tall and purple, it was much smaller than Mount

Olympus. But far scarier. Because the evil King Hephaestus's underground palace, er, *prison*, was there!

If only I had something that would help us on our quest or in battle, thought Persephone. Aphrodite had a chariot. Artemis, her bow and arrows. Heracles, his strength and club. And Athena had winged sandals that could fly her anywhere. For some reason they weren't working right now, but Athena was also very clever. She could probably come up with a great plan to help with their rescue attempt. But flowers weren't useful in a quest or in battle. So how could Persephone help?

2

Into the Mountain

In no time at all, Aphrodite's chariot drew near the king's island mountain.

Bang! Bang! Bang! A loud clanging sound made them all cover their ears. "Where's that awful noise coming from?" Aphrodite wondered aloud.

Built into the front wall of the mountain were two huge **bronze** doors. One moved left. The other moved right, both sliding sideways to open in opposite directions. ***Bang!*** Then they slid to

slam shut again. Over and over.

Persephone shuddered. "It's like a big mouth with teeth that chomp sideways instead of up and down."

"Yikes!" said Artemis. "I wouldn't want to be caught between them when those doors close!"

"Me neither," said Athena. "They were made to scare away visitors!"

Aphrodite guided her doves to land the chariot near the doors. Everyone hopped out. Then the doves flew the chariot to the top of the mountain to wait until needed.

Heracles frowned as they walked up to the slamming doors. "There should be a warning sign here."

"Yeah," said Persephone. "It should say, 'Beware of doors. You might get squished!'"

They all laughed.

Oliver had been sniffing around a pile of sticks near the doors. Now he began to bark at them. ***Woof! Woof!***

Suddenly the sticks took shape. A stick guy! It had eyes, arms, and legs! It raced off on its stick legs, leaping through the doors as they opened. Oliver ran after it.

"Oliver, no!" shouted Athena. Luckily, her little white dog made it inside the mountain—tail and

all—just in the nick of time. ***BANG!***

When the doors opened again, Athena zoomed through too.

"Athena, no!" yelled Persephone. "Wait for us!" But it was too late. ***BANG!*** The doors slammed shut behind Athena.

Heracles acted fast. The very next time the doors opened, he **wedged** his club between them. Then he, Aphrodite, Artemis, and Persephone quickly hopped over the club. Yellow Wing flew over it. When the doors slid apart again, Heracles grabbed his club back. ***BANG!*** The doors slammed together again. They were *all* inside the mountain now!

"Athena?" Persephone called out. "Oliver?"

But Athena didn't answer. And Oliver didn't bark.

"Ow!" said Persephone.

"Sorry for bumping into you," came Aphrodite's voice. "It's so dark in here. I can't see a thing!"

"Me neither," Artemis said near Persephone's other ear.

Just then the doors opened again and a little light got in. "Look!" said Artemis. "I think I see a tunnel ahead. It might lead us to Athena."

"Grab hands so no one gets lost," Heracles suggested.

"Yeah, and only walk when the doors are open and we can see," added Persephone.

"I'll lead," said Yellow Wing. "Since I'm an owl, I can see in the dark."

Holding hands, and with the

Owlie directing their steps, they went deeper into the mountain. They passed through an arched rock doorway. Then they entered a long hallway lit by gold lamps.

Now that they could see again, they dropped hands. At the end of the hall was a door. They opened it and peeked inside a large room.

It had a high ceiling shaped like an upside-down bowl. Two large beams crisscrossed below the dome. Yellow Wing flew up to sit on one of them as they all went inside.

"Look!" Persephone whispered. She pointed at a huge throne in the center of the room. Made of marble, it was covered with sparkly jewels.

Hearing a tapping sound, she and the others whirled around. A short, bearded man had come in behind them. He carried a shiny silver cane. ***Tap. Tap. Tap.***

"Welcome!" he called out. "I've been expecting you!" He tapped the floor with his cane as he walked across the room and sat upon the throne.

"Must be King Hephaestus," Heracles whispered to the others.

"Was it his crown that tipped you off?" asked Aphrodite. "I love the jewels in it!" No surprise, since she loved fancy things.

Persephone frowned. "Wait. He was expecting us? That stick guy

TAP
TAP

outside must have been a spy!"

Artemis stepped forward. "We've come for the queen," she boldly told the king. "We know you have her. You must let her go!"

The king raised an eyebrow. "Must I?" He grinned wide. "And I suppose you'll also want me to free your friend and her little dog?"

Persephone and the others gasped. "You've captured them, too?" Persephone exclaimed.

Heracles lifted his club to his

shoulder, as if ready to swing into action.

The king eyed the club calmly. “Yup. My palace, my rules.” He waved his silver cane in the air like a magic wand. **“Army, arise!”** he commanded.

A dozen gold doors suddenly appeared along the walls of the room. And dozens of the stick guys marched in through them. They were dressed in shining armor and carried spears and swords. And they looked fierce.

Persephone's heart sank. She had expected they might face a battle. But not against such a large and well-equipped army as this! Even Heracles was surprised as he let his club drop to his side.

3 Games

"Give up?" King Hephaestus patted his belly and smiled an evil smile. "Might as well. You cannot fight me and win," he told Persephone and her friends. "I am too powerful."

"Just let your prisoners go. Nobody wants a battle," Aphrodite told him.

That isn't quite true, thought Persephone. She was sure that her friends—including Aphrodite—would gladly fight this king and his army. Anything to rescue Athena, Oliver, and the queen! There had to be some way to free them!

"We could make a trade," she suggested. "You free the queen, our friend, and her dog. And we'll give you something in return."

"Humph," said the king. "I have more treasure than you can ever imagine. The sticks serve me as soldiers and spies. Plus, they work day and night mining silver and gold and jewels. And now, with the queen as my prisoner, I'm even more powerful. What else could I need?"

"How about a chariot drawn by doves?" offered Aphrodite.

What a great idea! thought Persephone. That was sooo nice of Aphrodite. Persephone wished *she* had something she could offer in trade.

But the king said, "Bah! Chariot schmariot. I never leave my underground palace. Why would I need a chariot? I don't like the world outside my mountain."

Persephone and her friends stared at the king in surprise. "Then why do you want to rule it?" Artemis asked.

The king blinked. "Because it's fun to be the boss. And I can rule this island perfectly well from here.

If I need something done, I just send one of my stick guys to do it."

Heracles frowned. "But a ruler should go out among the people and talk to them. See what help they might need."

"Help?" The king started laughing. "It's their job to help me, not the other way around. Besides, if they wanted to ask for help, they could enter my mountain."

"What? And get crushed by those sliding doors trying to get in?" Aphrodite blurted out.

The king shrugged. "Those doors are a hoot, right? Makes getting inside kind of a game!"

"Ha!" said Artemis. "Some game. Since you never leave your palace, it's a game you can't lose!"

"True. That's the best kind of game!" the king exclaimed. He stroked his beard. "Would you all like to play a game right now?"

"Huh? What kind of game?" Persephone asked, curious. "If we win it, will you let your prisoners go free?"

"Sure," said the king. "But don't count on winning."

"We'll try, though," Persephone said. What else could they do?

"First, let us see the queen and Athena, so we know they're okay," Aphrodite said.

The king laughed. "But that's the game! You have to find them!"

"But aren't they locked in a prison?" asked Heracles.

"No. Not the kind you imagine, anyway. Come!" With that, the king leaped from his throne. He waved his silver cane and another door appeared. A green door this time, covered in emeralds.

"Wow!" Persephone couldn't help saying. Green was her favorite color, the color of *plants*.

"Follow me!" the king said.

4

Hidden Treasures

Before he led them through the green door, however, he waved his cane again. At once, his army of sticks marched back out through the gold doors. He also made Heracles leave his club, and

Artemis, her bow and arrows, in the throne room. Yellow Wing was left behind on the high beam overhead.

Persephone and her friends entered a new room. This one had walls and floors of polished marble. An arched ceiling rose far above their heads.

The room was stuffed with small tables of different shapes and sizes. Some were made from carved woods, others from marble or glass. On top of each table sat small treasures. There were jeweled necklaces and rings. There were gold and silver dishes. There were tiny crystal animal statues, glass vases and bowls, toys, and many other things. A soft glow lit the room, making the objects sparkle.

"Now this is more like it. Fancy!" said Aphrodite.

"It's like a **museum**," Artemis said.

"Indeed," said the king. "But not all of the objects in this room are what they appear to be."

"Huh?" said Heracles. "What's that mean?"

"The queen, your friend Athena, and her dog are all hidden here," the king told them. "**I changed them into treasures!** Awesome, right?" He rubbed his hands together in delight. "Now, only one of you gets to play my game. Who will it be? Who will guess which of my treasures are actually the friends you seek?"

Persephone and her friends looked at one another. "So if the player guesses right, you'll free Athena and the others?" Artemis asked the king.

"Yes, of course," said the king. "I'll give the player seven guesses. If they get even one guess right, they get seven *more* guesses!"

"But there are hundreds of treasures here!" Aphrodite objected.

"Even with fourteen guesses total we'd have to be really lucky to find Athena, Oliver, and the queen."

King Hephaestus folded his arms. "Like I said, my palace. **My rules.** Now, which one of you will play?"

"If Athena were here, she'd be the best choice," said Heracles. "She's the smartest."

"But she's not here," noted Aphrodite. "So . . ."

Suddenly, Persephone's friends were all looking at her. Or actually at the four-leaf clovers in her hair.

"Your clovers are good luck. That gives you the best chance at guessing right," Artemis said, pointing at them.

Aphrodite and Heracles nodded.

Persephone gulped. "Um. All right," she said. She just hoped that that her good luck would work in this dark place. Because her four-leaf clovers (and flowers as well) were beginning to sag.

"Great!" said the king. "But before you start guessing, I need to explain the rest of the rules."

"Rest of the rules?" Persephone repeated.

The king grinned at her and her friends. "Don't you want to know what will happen if you *don't* guess correctly?"

"We have to leave without freeing anyone?" Persephone guessed. It was too horrible to imagine!

"Wrong." The king jabbed his cane in her and her friends' direction. "If you fail to guess all three, I'll turn the four of you into treasures too! The more prisoners, the better." He let out an evil laugh.

At this, everybody gasped. But then Heracles began to spin in circles. "Ooh. Look what I can do!" he called out. "I'd make a cool top in the museum, don't you think?"

This made them laugh, even the king.

"It won't happen," Aphrodite said firmly. "I trust in Persephone's good luck."

"Me too," said Artemis.

Persephone's stomach tightened.

Her friends might trust in her luck, but she wasn't sure *she* could. Becoming an object in the king's treasure museum would be terrible! But they had to play his awful game. Otherwise they'd have no chance of freeing Athena, the queen, and Oliver. They couldn't leave them behind!

She reached up to touch one of her four-leaf clovers. **Oh no!** It felt floppy. "Perk up!" she whispered to it. But it didn't. It needed sunlight. She tried not to worry as she began to walk among the tables. There was no choice. She would have to hope her clovers could still bring her good luck.

The king had posted a half-dozen stick guards around her three friends, so they couldn't help her guess. He followed her, tapping his cane now and then.

Persephone looked carefully at the treasures on a marble table. *Could that yellow crystal lion be the queen?* she wondered. Lions were a **symbol** of royalty.

She pointed to it. “Is this the queen?”

The king laughed. **“No!”** He twirled his cane happily. “One guess down, six more to go.”

“Unless she guesses correctly,” Heracles called out to remind him. “Then she gets seven more guesses.”

“Yes, sure. Like that’s going to happen,” said the king. He rolled his eyes. ***Tap, tap, tap***, went his cane.

For her next guess, Persephone chose a pretty blue bowl. It was the same color as Athena's eyes.

"Wrong again!" the king exclaimed. He rubbed his hands together and grinned.

Persephone made three more guesses. A crystal dog that she hoped might be Oliver. A purple vase she thought might be the queen, because purple was a royal color.

And a necklace with a gold slipper charm. It made her think of Athena's winged sandals.

"Wrong. Wrong. And wrong!" the king told her gleefully.

Her good luck wasn't working! Her clovers were too weak. Her hand shook as she pointed to her sixth and next-to-last guess. It was a jeweled pin in the shape of a sailboat. She chose it because Athena had come to this island on a boat.

"Ha! Wrong again!" the king announced.

Persephone groaned. "I'm sorry!" she called to her friends.

"You still have one more guess," said Aphrodite.

"You can do it!"

Artemis added. "Think smart."

"Take your time," Heracles encouraged. "I was kidding when I said I'd make a cool top. None of us want to become objects in this museum!"

Persephone nodded, worried. She looked around, trying to think smart. But the king's tapping was making it hard. She stared closely at each treasure as she circled the tables again and again. ***Tap, tap, tap***, went the king's silver cane as he followed her around.

Suddenly, Persephone noticed he was tapping tables, not the floor. The *same three tables* each time. Could those be the tables with enchanted treasures? Maybe he didn't realize he was giving hints. Or maybe it was his idea of a mean joke!

From the corner of her eye she watched him tap one of the three tables he'd tapped before. His eyes slid toward a pretty silver bell with a carved wooden handle.

Aha! she thought.

"Hurry up," the king complained. "You're taking too much time. Just choose something!"

"Okay. I choose this," said Persephone. Hoping she was right, she picked up the silver bell and rang it.

Instantly the bell flew from

her hand. It **transformed** into the figure of a tall silver-haired woman. The queen!

"Hooray!" Persephone's friends cheered.

But King Hephaestus almost dropped his cane in surprise.

"What's going on here?" the queen asked. Her voice was similar to the tone of the bell, Persephone noticed. And that gave her an idea. A *sound* (as in, both noisy and smart) idea.

"Shh!" the king said to

the queen. "We're in the middle of a game here." He watched Persephone move to the second of the tables he'd tapped with his cane.

"A game?" the queen repeated.

Heracles pushed past two stick guy guards and went to her. "The king turned you into a silver bell," he began explaining as the stick guards caught up to him. They herded him and the queen over to where the others were standing.

Meanwhile, Persephone's eye fell on a golden whistle. It was the only item on the second table that could produce a sound.

She picked it up and blew on it. It made a sharp **tweet** that matched the pitch of Oliver's barking. Right away the whistle flew from Persephone's mouth. It turned back into Athena's little dog.

Woof! Woof! Oliver ran to Artemis, who picked him up and hugged him.

Now Persephone raced to the third table the king had tapped. This time she didn't need luck to guide her guess. She grabbed two small bronze **cymbals** and clanged them together. As the cymbals fell from her hands, Athena magically appeared.

5
The Silver Cane

Persephone hugged Athena. "We were worried we'd never see you again!" she exclaimed.

"We won!" Heracles whooped, doing a happy dance. He and the others broke free of the guards and came over.

Athena looked confused. "What happened? Where are we? Won what?" she asked. She had no idea that she and Oliver had been objects in the king's museum only moments before.

"The king changed you into cymbals," Aphrodite told her. "And turned Oliver into a golden whistle! The queen was a bell." Then she explained how Persephone had freed all three by correctly guessing which treasures they were.

Aphrodite and Artemis joined Persephone and Athena in a group hug. Oliver jumped around them happily.

With a sour look on his face, the king stomped out the green door. Persephone and the others, including the six stick guys, followed him back into the throne room. Artemis grabbed her bow and arrows, and Heracles his club.

"Rules changed!" the king announced suddenly. "I'm not letting you go after all!"

He waved his cane over his head. It was a magical call for his army of stick guys!

Tink! Blink! Just then, a blinking light appeared above the king's throne.

"Hestia!" said Persephone. She pointed to the place where the tiny, flying goddess now hovered.

Hestia did an air curtsy to the queen. "I'm glad to see you're back to your usual self, Your Highness." Then she frowned at the king. "Because you've used your cane for evil, you've lost the right to keep it."

At her command, Yellow Wing swooped down from the ceiling beam. He'd been there the whole time. The Owlie tugged away the king's silver cane with both claws.

"Give it back!" the king yelled in surprise. He hopped up and

down, trying to reach his cane. But Yellow Wing flew away with it.

"That cane has magic powers," Hestia told Persephone and her friends. "Just like Athena's winged sandals. It must never be returned to King Hephaestus."

"But without my cane, how will I rule the stick guys?" the king whined. "They might refuse to serve me! They might even leave my army. And then the **islanders** won't be scared of me."

At this, the ears of the half-dozen stick guy guards in the room perked up.

"Good! Maybe you should try treating everyone with kindness!" Aphrodite blurted out.

"Exactly," said the queen. "Try helping others for a change!"

The king rolled his eyes. "Kind schmind. Where's the fun in that?"

"Why do you even need an army?" Artemis asked him.

"Yeah," said Athena, who was holding Oliver now. "Has your palace ever actually been attacked? Do you have enemies?"

The king's face turned red. "Well, no, but I still want my cane back. It shows I'm the boss."

"Never," Hestia told him firmly. The tiny goddess looked at the queen. "The cane would be safe in your hands, I think."

"Thank you," said the queen. "But I don't need a magic cane to rule well and with kindness."

The queen smiled at Persephone. "From what Heracles has told me, I owe my freedom to you."

"So do we," Athena said, pointing to herself and Oliver.

Hestia smiled at Persephone. "Maybe you should have the cane."

"Yes!" Persephone's friends and the queen called out.

"No!" the king roared. But he was outvoted.

At once, Yellow Wing flew down from the beam with the magic cane. Opening its claws, the Owlie dropped the silver cane into Persephone's hands.

"Wow! Thank you!" She smiled

at the others. **“Lucky me!”**

They all laughed, except for the king. He just gave her a dark look.

But really, thought Persephone, *it isn’t luck that helped me win the game.* Her four-leaf clovers had been too weak to aid her guesses.

She'd figured out what the king was up to on her own. It was just the sort of brainy thinking Athena might have done. That is, if she hadn't been cymbals at the time!

"Remember, you must use the cane's magic only for good," Hestia told her.

Persephone smiled. "I will."

Hestia's light began to blink faster. It was a sure sign that she would soon disappear. Her comings and goings were never truly under her control, it seemed.

"About my winged sandals," Athena said to her hurriedly. "They've lost their powers. Or at least they don't work on this island. Can you tell me how to get home without them? Now that our quest to free the queen is over? I arrived in a boat, but it floated away and sank, so I—"

"You must recharge them," Hestia interrupted her to say quickly. "Persephone can help. She can use her cane to—" ***Pop!*** She was gone.

6

Journey's End

"The islanders will be worried about me," the queen said once Hestia had disappeared. "I need to get back to my palace to let them know I'm okay." She glanced side-ways at the king. "I also need to tell them they're no longer in danger from stick soldiers, spies, and evil magic. Without your silver cane, you have no real power to make anyone do anything they don't want to do."

At this, the faces of the six stick guards broke into smiles.

"Really? Then I quit!" one of them said.

"Me too!" exclaimed the others. And they walked away, whistling.

King Hephaestus became crabby. "Everything's ruined now.

Just go away," he said to the queen and her rescuers.

So they did. Beyond the lamp-lit passageway, they came to the mountain's exit. ***BANG!*** The doors slammed shut. Then open again. Then shut.

"Just a minute. I'll jam them," Heracles said, holding his club sideways.

"Wait," said Persephone. "Let me try something." She waved her new cane in the air the way she'd seen the king do it. **"Open!"**

she commanded the doors. "And stay open until everyone is out!"

The doors obeyed. In seconds, she and her friends stood outside. They'd escaped the mountain! In the sunlight now, her flowers and clovers grew straight and strong again. **Hooray!**

Aphrodite whistled for her chariot. The doves flew down with it, and everyone piled in. Aphrodite and Heracles sat in front with the queen. Persephone, Athena, and Artemis took the back seat. Yellow Wing sat on Athena's shoulder, while Oliver curled up in her lap.

As the golden chariot sailed into the air, Artemis looked longingly at Persephone's silver cane. "I wish I had a magical object like that. Or like Athena's winged sandals."

Her words made Persephone remember how she'd wished for things the others had too. Things she thought would be useful in battle or during their quest. As it turned out, she hadn't needed anything but her own smart thinking to best the king. Maybe the next time she wished for something someone else had, she'd try to remember that.

"What would you do with a cane like Persephone's?" Athena asked Artemis.

She grinned. "I'd turn King Hephaestus into an object in his own museum!"

Athena and Persephone laughed. "That would serve him right," Athena said.

Privately, Persephone agreed. But she had promised Hestia to only use the cane's magic for good. And she would keep that promise.

At last the chariot reached the queen's palace on the top of a hill. A crowd of islanders was waiting when the chariot landed. They cheered when they saw her.

After everyone climbed down from the chariot, Heracles agreed to stay and help the queen. It was important for things to get back to normal on the island, so that the islanders could return to their usual activities. With a cheerful wave to the goddess girls, Heracles and the queen headed for the palace.

The four goddess girls stood near the chariot. "I wish Hestia had finished telling us how your

cane could make my sandals work again," Athena told Persephone.

"Maybe we can figure it out." Persephone waved the silver cane in the air. "Recharge Athena's sandals so they can fly!" she commanded.

Athena's face brightened. But the wings at her heels stayed still.

"Try again," Artemis suggested.

"Maybe tap the sandals?" added Aphrodite.

"Good idea!" Persephone remembered how the king kept

tapping his cane on the tables containing the bell, whistle, and cymbals. She'd wondered again if there had been a different reason he was doing it, or if he had done it as a joke. But maybe he'd *had* to do it. To recharge the objects' enchantment!

Reaching out with her cane, she tapped one of Athena's sandals

and then the other. Instantly, their wings began to flap. They lifted Athena a few inches above the ground, and then set her down again. Their power was back!

Athena beamed at her. **"You did it!"**

"Hooray!" exclaimed Artemis and Aphrodite.

Persephone smiled. But then she felt sad. "Will you fly home right away, Athena? I was hoping you'd come back to Mount Olympus with us."

Athena thought for a moment. "I *would* like to see Sparkle City again. And spend more time with you all . . ."

"Then come!" said Aphrodite.

"Please," added Artemis.

Athena grinned. "Okay! I guess I can stay a bit longer. After all, hardly any time at all will have passed since I left my home. Time in this magic land moves much more quickly!"

"Yay!" shouted Persephone. She gave her new cane a happy twirl.

The four friends hugged one another happily. This quest might be at an end, but a new adventure was surely just around the corner!

Word List

bronze (BRAWNZ): A metal made from copper and tin

chariot (CHAIR•ee•ut): A two-wheeled cart drawn by animals (usually horses) in ancient times

cymbals (SIHM•bulls): Two flat, round disks that make a noise when clapped together

enchantress (en•CHAN•tress): A woman who practices magic and casts spells

fierce (FEERS): Powerfully strong

goddess (GOD•ess): A girl or woman with magic powers in Greek mythology

islanders (EYE•land•erz): The people who live on an island

Mount Olympus (MOWNT oh•LIHM•puhss): Tallest mountain in Greece

museum (mew•ZEE•um): A building/room where interesting objects are on display

quiver (QWIV•er): A bag for arrows

Sparkle City (SPAR•kuhl SIHT•ee): City at the top of Mount Olympus

symbol (SIHM•bull): A thing that represents or stands for something else

transformed (trans•FORMD): Went through a big change

tweet (TWEET): A short, high-pitched sound

wedged (WEHJD): Fixed into position with the use of an object

Questions

1. Persephone wishes she had something like Aphrodite's chariot, Heracles's club, or Artemis's bow and arrows. Things that would be helpful in battle or in the friends' quest. Can you describe a time you wished for something someone else had, and how you felt not having that thing?
2. What were your feelings about King Hephaestus when you first met him in the story? Did your feelings about him change by the

end of the book? Why or why not?

3. Do you think most of the stick guys will continue to serve the king even after he loses his magic silver cane? Why or why not?
4. What things happen in the story that help Persephone finally figure out which objects in the king's museum are actually the queen, Athena, and Oliver?
5. Do you think Persephone will be able to keep her promise to Hestia to only use the magic silver cane for good? Why or why not?

Authors' Note

Some of the ideas in the Little Goddess Girls books come from Greek mythology. Like Persephone's special love for plants. She was the goddess of spring and growing things! We also borrowed a few ideas from *Ozma of Oz*, the third book in the Oz series written by L. Frank Baum. While there are some similarities, we've added a lot of action and our own ideas to this story. We hope you enjoy reading the Little Goddess Girls books!

—Joan Holub and Suzanne Williams